静

和

南禅寺大佛殿唐塑

THE TANG SCULPTURES IN THE GREAT BUDDHA HALL OF NANCHAN TEMPLE

山西省古建筑与彩塑壁画保护研究院

三晋出版社 编

山西出版传媒集团

三晋出版社

影

光

南禅寺位于山西省五台县阳白乡李家庄村西侧岗峦上。寺院坐北朝南,占地面积 4158 平方米,由东、西两个院落构成。位于西院的大佛殿为唐代建筑,其他建筑为明、清所建。大佛殿初创年代已不可确考,从殿内现存大梁墨书题记看,重建于唐建中三年(782),为中国现存最古老的木结构建筑,也是国内唯一尚存的唐武宗"会昌灭法"之前的木构佛教殿宇建筑。

首先,大佛殿内原有唐建中年间重建时绘塑的彩塑 17 身,现存 14 身。此坛彩塑自唐建中三年塑绘完成后,虽经后世数次补塑、重装,但仍然保存了唐代彩塑原有的题材内容和样式风格。

1. 盛中唐之际以丰腴为美的造像风格尚存。此坛彩塑,除迦叶造像外,其余佛、菩萨、天王、善财及阿难造像,均面相丰盈、肢体健硕、耳大垂肩,与敦煌莫高窟等盛中唐佛教造像的样式风格基本一致。此外,坛上四尊立式菩萨均做 S 形站姿,是印度帕拉菩萨造像样式对中国唐代菩萨造像影响的例证。

2. 唐代流行的穿着、装饰犹存。坛上立式菩萨上身袒露，项佩璎珞，胸前斜扎络腋，肩绕披帛，脐下系短裙，下着贴腿窄裤，跣足。头上青丝均挽作高髻，旁插钿花装饰。此种穿着、装饰，受印度笈多、帕拉造像影响，是唐代菩萨衣饰的主要特征，与莫高窟、麦积山等处唐代菩萨造像颇为相近。

3. 唐代重要纹饰图案基本保存。坛上释迦牟尼佛右侧塑有一尊立式菩萨，腰系短裙，右胯短裙上面现存一幅童子坐卧画面；坛上释迦牟尼佛身后背光上，现存山石、水波、树木、云朵等图案，大多属于唐代塑绘的原有题材内容。据此可知，此坛塑像虽经后世补塑、重装，外层图案色彩已有所改动，与原塑不尽相同，但一些重要的图案画面题材内容，仍然较好地保存和传承下来，实为珍贵。

4. 唐代须弥座基本保持原样。佛坛中央释迦牟尼佛所坐须弥座，横切面为等边六棱形。束腰以上叠涩、上枋部分，被须弥座上铺设的双重座幔垂搭遮掩，仅有两身摩羯鱼首露出；束腰两侧，各置蜀柱一根；束腰正中棱面与两侧棱面交汇处，各塑侧卧力士一身，呈肩膀奋力抬扛须弥座状；正中置一壸门，壸门正中塑置青鬃金毛狮子一身；束腰下有叠涩三层,中间一层做覆莲状;叠涩下置须弥基座,基座与最下一层叠涩间再做一层束腰,每一个棱面交汇处仍置小蜀柱一根。佛直接坐于须弥座上,而不再于须弥座上置莲座,是中晚唐五台山及周边地区佛座制作的基本样式。此样式之主要特点,在五台山佛光寺东大殿佛坛中央释迦牟尼佛所坐须弥座上有同样体现。

其次,此坛唐塑在中国古代佛教造像史乃至思想史上有重要价值和意义,主要表现在以下几个方面:

1. 此坛唐塑是中国内地目前所知塑绘年代最早的一坛泥质彩绘造像遗存。也是目前所见制作时间最早的一坛"华严三圣"造像。几乎可以肯定,南禅寺不会是"华严三圣"的始创寺院,有可能仅是对五台山地区开风气之先的名寺、大寺的模仿或跟进。但此坛造像仍为后人认识和研究中唐之际五台山及中原地区的华严造像提供了实物依据。

2. 由身着螺旋纹铠甲的骑狮文殊及于阗王、善财童子构成的组像,是国内所见制作时间最早的"护国文殊"和"新样文殊"遗存。当然,此组造像亦应非南禅寺首创，或也是模仿、借鉴五台山其他名寺、大寺题材样式而成，但同样为我们认识和探讨中唐以降文殊题材造像乃至文殊信仰变化提供了实物依据。

3. 大佛殿佛坛善财参访摩耶夫人的造像，是大乘佛教的"菩萨行"思想和实践，通过"像教"方式的又一精彩表述和体现，也是印度大乘佛教思想与中国传统文化精华结合后，佛教造像进一步中国化的又一生动例证。

Nanchan Temple is located on the hill to the west of Lijiazhuang Village, Yangbai Town, Wutai County, Shanxi Province. The temple faces south and covers an area of 4158 square meters, consisting of two courtyards in the east and the west. The Great Buddha Hall in the west courtyard was constructed in Tang Dynasty, while the rest of the temple was built in Ming and Qing dynasties. It is not exactly clear when the Great Buddha Hall was first established. According to an inscription found on the beam, the hall was rebuilt in the third year of Jianzhong Reign, Tang Dynasty (782 CE), thus making it the oldest extant wooden structure in China as well as the only wooden Buddhist structure that survived the "Huichang Persecution of Buddhism" movement initiated by Emperor Wuzong of Tang Dynasty.

Firstly, 14 of the original 17 painted statues created during the Jianzhong years' reconstruction have survived and managed to maintain their original subject content and decorative styles even though they have gone through numerous restorations and redecorations during the following centuries.

1. The high Tang style that favored the beauty of plumpness is still visible. Except for the statue of Kasyapa, all the other statues including Buddha, Bodhisattvas, Heavenly Kings, Sudhana and Ananda appear as buxom and strong figures, which is highly consistent with the high Tang style found in the Mogao Grottoes of Dunhuang. Additionally, the four standing Bodhisattvas on the altar all stand in a posture that

shows a S-curve of the torso, which is a clear example of the influence that Indian Buddhist sculpture of Pala Dynasty had on the Tang Buddhist art.

2. Popular styles of clothing and decoration from Tang Dynasty can be observed in the statues. The standing Bodhisattvas on the altar are all bare-chested, wearing wreaths on the neck, wrapping long shawls around the shoulders, short gowns and narrow trousers and barefoot. The hairs were tied up in a high bun, decorated with jewels and flowers. This type of clothing and decoration was one of the most fashionable in Tang sculptures of Bodhisattvas, largely influenced by the India art of Gupta and Pala periods, and very similar cases can also be found in the Tang Bodhisattva statues of Mogao Grottoes and Maijishan Grottoes.

3. Important decorative patterns of Tang Dynasty can be basically observed. The standing Bodhisattva on the altar beside Sakyamuni wears a short gown, which preserves an image of a young boy on its right crotch; the background halo of Sakyamuni on the altar preserves patterns of mountain rocks, water waves, trees, clouds and so on mostly belonging to a typical Tang repertoire. Based on this observation, one can conclude that although the statues on the altar have gone through numerous restorations and redecorations, and the outer layer color themes might have been changed and far removed from the original, but quite some important patterns and subjects have still been well preserved and inherited by the later generations, which makes the statues all the more

important and valuable.

4. The Tang Sumeru Thrones are largely kept intact. The Sumeru Throne where Sakyamuni is seated in the center of the altar has a transverse section of equilateral hexagon. The corbel, upper fillet and fascia above the central waist of the Sumeru Throne is partially concealed by the seat covers hanging from the throne seat, with only the heads of two Makaras reaching out; there are king posts on each side, and throne supporters on each corner of the central waist; in the center of the central waist there is an arched gate, under which a statue of golden lion with dark mane is seated; under the central waist there are three steps of corbels, with the middle step appearing as upside-down lotus petals; below the corbel steps and above the foundation there is another waist, with minor king posts on each side. The Buddha is sitting directly on the Sumeru Throne, instead of on a lotus platform on top of the throne, and this is the way how Buddha throne was arranged in the Mt. Wutai region during the middle and late Tang Dynasty. A similar arrangement could be found in the Sakyamuni Buddha throne on the central altar of the East Main Hall, Foguang Temple.

Secondly, the sculpture group here is of great value and significance in the history of Buddhist statues in ancient China and even in the history of Buddhist thought.

1. The sculpture group is the earliest extant example of the Avatamsaka Trinity statues. Nanchan Temple is most certain-

ly not the monastery where the Avatamsaka Trinity image was first established, and probably in creating this sculpture group it was just trying to catch up with the trend initiated in other more significant monasteries in the region. However, it is the earliest extant example of this tradition which makes it an important concrete evidence for studying the mid-Tang Avatamsaka iconography in the region.

2. The Great Buddha Hall sculpture group of Manjusri riding a lion in armor with spiral patterns, the King of Khotan, and Sudhanakumara, is the earliest extant example of the so-called "protector Manjusri" and "new-style Manjusri" in China. Again, this new style of Manjusri image is probably not first established here in Nanchan Temple, and probably in creating this group it was just trying to catch up with the trend in the region. But it is still an important piece of evidence for studying the mid-Tang Manjusri iconography and its development.

3. The sculpture group of Sudhanakumara visiting Mahamaya Devi on the altar of the Great Buddha Hall is another wonderful expression and embodiment of "Bodhisattva-carya" (the Practices of Bodhisattva) in Mahayana Buddhism thoughts and practices through "image preaching". This is an example of the localization of Buddhism in the form of statues after a hybridization of Indian Mahayana Buddhism with Chinese traditional cultures.

南禅寺大佛殿唐塑分布示意图

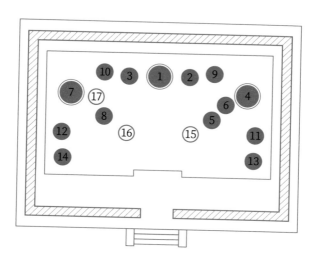

1 释迦牟尼佛 / 毗卢遮那佛像
2 迦叶像
3 阿难像
4 乘象普贤像
5 乘象普贤右侧善财童子像
6 乘象普贤右侧驭象人像
7 骑狮文殊像
8 骑狮文殊左侧善财童子像
9 佛左后侧胁侍菩萨像

10 佛右后侧胁侍菩萨像
11 佛左前侧胁侍菩萨像
12 佛右前侧胁侍菩萨像
13 佛前侧护法天王像
14 佛前侧护法天王像
15 佛前左侧供养菩萨像（已失）
16 佛前右侧供养菩萨像（已失）
17 于阗王像（已失）

释迦牟尼佛 / 毗卢遮那佛像

The Statue of Sakyamuni / Vairocana Buddha
(Height 3.91m)

佛坛须弥座

The Sumeru Throne

迦叶像

The Statue of Kasyapa
(Height 1.99m)

迦叶像

The Statue of Kasyapa
(Height 1.99m)

阿难像

The Statue of Ananda Buddha
(Height 2.15m)

阿难像

The Statue of Ananda Buddha
(Height 2.15m)

乘象普贤像

The Statue of Samantabhadra
Bodhisattva on an Elephant
(Height 3.05m)

普贤菩萨坐骑白象

Mount of Samantabhadra: White Elephant

乘象普贤右侧善财童子像

The Statue of Sudhanakumara on the Right
Side of Samantabhadra Bodhisattva
(Height 1.01m)

乘象普贤右侧驭象人像

The Statue of the Elephant Attendant on the
Right Side of Samantabhadra Bodhisattva
(Height 1.25m)

乘象普贤右侧驭象人像

The Statue of the Elephant Attendant on the
Right Side of Samantabhadra Bodhisattva
(Height 1.25m)

骑狮文殊像

The Statue of Manjusri Bodhisattva on a Lion
(Height 3.05m)

骑狮文殊像

The Statue of Manjusri Bodhisattva on a Lion
(Height 3.05m)

骑狮文殊左侧善财童子像

The Statue of Sudhanakumara on the
Left Side of Manjusri Bodhisattva
(Height 1.00m)

佛左后侧胁侍菩萨像

The Statue of the Acolyte Bodhisattva on
the Left Rear of Sakyamuni Buddha
(Height 2.44m)

佛左后侧胁侍菩萨像

The Statue of the Acolyte Bodhisattva on
the Left Rear of Sakyamuni Buddha
(Height 2.44m)

佛右后侧胁侍菩萨像

The Statue of the Acolyte Bodhisattva on
the Right Rear of Sakyamuni Buddha
(Height 2.41m)

佛右后侧胁侍菩萨像

The Statue of the Acolyte Bodhisattva on
the Right Rear of Sakyamuni Buddha
(Height 2.41m)

佛左前侧胁侍菩萨像

The Statue of the Acolyte Bodhisattva on
Left Front of Sakyamuni Buddha
(Height 2.69m)

佛左前侧胁侍菩萨像

The Statue of the Acolyte Bodhisattva on
Left Front of Sakyamuni Buddha
(Height 2.69m)

佛右前侧胁侍菩萨像

The Statue of the Acolyte Bodhisattva on
Right Front of Sakyamuni Buddha
(Height 2.62m)

佛右前侧胁侍菩萨像

The Statue of the Acolyte Bodhisattva on
Right Front of Sakyamuni Buddha
(Height 2.62m)

佛左前侧护法天王像

The Statue of the Heavenly Guardian King
on Left Front of Sakyamuni Buddha
(Height 2.91m)

佛左前侧护法天王像

The Statue of the Heavenly Guardian King
on Left Front of Sakyamuni Buddha
(Height 2.91m)

护法天王与胁侍菩萨像

The Statue of a Heavenly Guardian King
and an Acolyte Bodhisattva

佛右前侧护法天王像

The Statue of the Heavenly Guardian King
on Right Front of Sakyamuni Buddha
(Height 2.78m)

佛前左侧供养菩萨像（已失）

The Statue of the Offering Bodhisattva
on Left Front of Sakyamuni (lost)

佛前右侧供养菩萨像（已失）

The Statue of the Offering Bodhisattva
on Right Front of Sakyamuni (lost)

于阗王像 (已失)

The Statue of the King of khotan (lost)